# In the Hot, Hot Sun

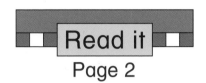

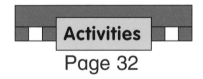

In the hot, hot sun, there was a tall, tall tree.

By the tall, tall tree, there was a black, black ant.

Near the black, black ant, there was a sweet, sweet rose.

By the sweet, sweet rose, there was a
brown, brown rock.

Near the brown, brown rock, there was a
huge, huge cave.

Read it

In the huge, huge cave, there was a big, big egg.

On the big, big egg, there was a little, little crack.

Run! It is a SNAKE!

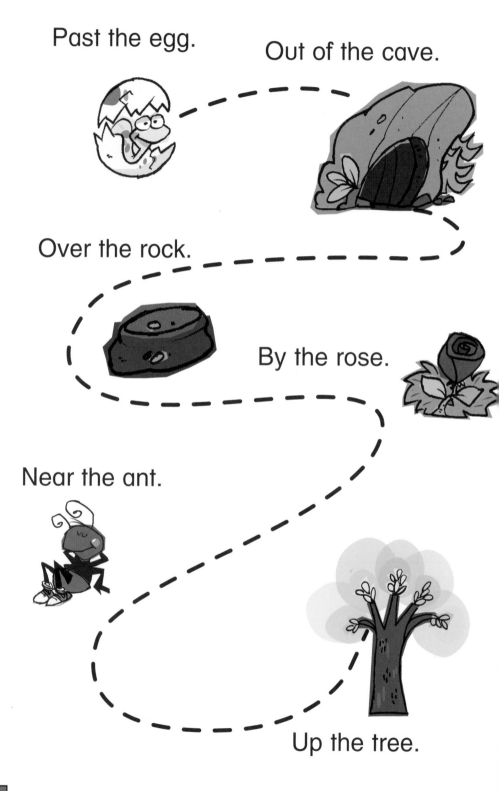

Past the egg.

Out of the cave.

Over the rock.

By the rose.

Near the ant.

Up the tree.

Safe at last in the hot, hot sun!

In the hot, hot _____,

there was a tall, tall

_____ .

By the tall, _____

tree, there was a black,

black _____.

Near the black, _____

ant, there was a sweet,

sweet _____.

By the _____ ,

sweet rose, there was

a brown, brown

_____ .

Near the brown,

_____

_____ rock,

there was a huge, huge

_____ .

In the huge, _____

cave, there was a big,

big _____.

On the big, _____

egg, there was a little,

_____ crack.

_____

_____!

It is a _____!

Past the _____ .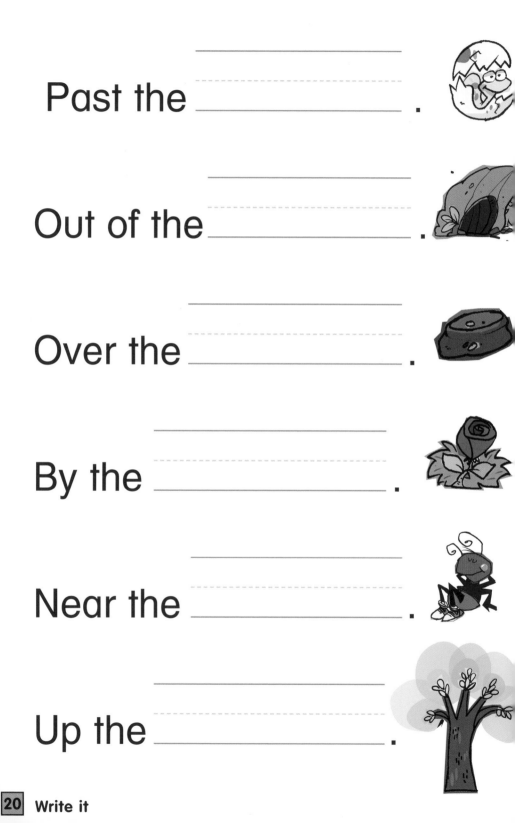

Out of the_____ .

Over the _____ .

By the _____ .

Near the _____ .

Up the _____ .

_____

Safe at _____ in

the hot, hot _____!

In the hot, hot sun, there was a tall, tall tree.

By the tall, tall tree, there was a black, black ant.

Near the black, black ant, there was a
sweet, sweet rose.

By the sweet, sweet rose, there was a brown, brown rock.

Near the brown, brown rock, there was a huge, huge cave.

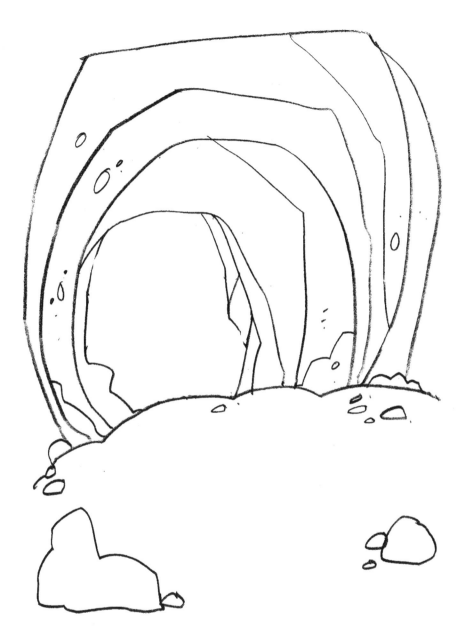

In the huge, huge cave, there was a big, big egg.

On the big, big egg, there was a little,
little crack.

Run! It is a SNAKE!

Past the egg.

Out of the cave.

Over the rock.

By the rose.

Near the ant.

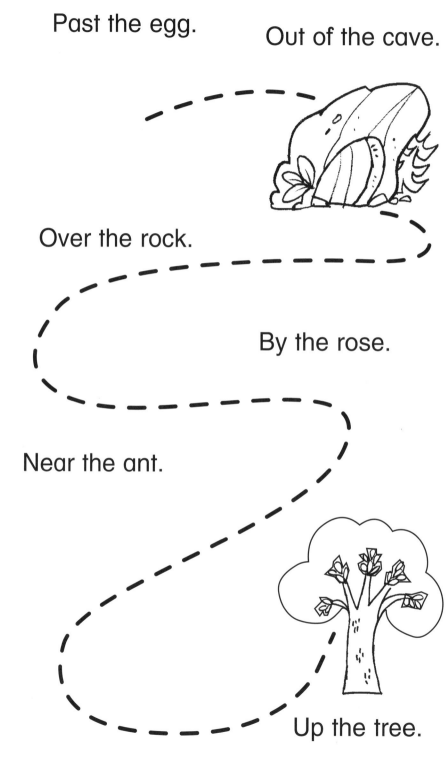

Up the tree.

Safe at last in the hot, hot sun!

# Activities

### Read it

Make your own books! Choose a subject that is of particular interest to the child. Then, if he or she is working on reading specific sight words, make learning to read those words the goal for your book. To create your book, staple pieces of paper together and paste a picture on each page. Then, write an easy-to-read sentence. Think of a title, and you will have created a book that your child will love to read again and again.

### Write it

Write a letter to a character! After your child or student has read a book, have him or her practice letter writing by writing a letter to a character from the book. Encourage him or her to ask questions and express opinions about the events in the book. Not only will you see your child or student blossom in his or her use of language and self-expression, you will also get a great peek into his or her comprehension of the book—without asking a single question.

### Draw it

Draw three scenes! Cut a large piece of paper into three equal sections, and then ask the child to think about what happened at the beginning, in the middle, and at the end of the story. Have him or her use the three pieces of paper to draw a picture to represent each part of the story. Finally, have the child retell (or summarize) the book by using his or her pictures as a guide!

A NOTE TO PARENTS:
When children create their own spellings for words they don't know, they are using **inventive spelling**. For the beginner, the act of writing is more important than the correctness of form. Sounding out words and predicting how they will be spelled reinforces an understanding of the connection between letters and sounds. Eventually, through experimenting with spelling patterns and repeated exposure to standard spelling, children will learn and use the correct form in their own writing. Until then, inventive spelling encourages early experimentation and self-expression in writing and nurtures a child's confidence as a writer.